My dear mouse friends,

Have I ever told you how much I love science fiction? I've always wanted to write incredible adventures set in another dimension, but I've never believed that parallel universes exist . . . until now!

That's because my good friend Professor Paws von Volt, the brilliant, secretive scientist, has just made an incredible discovery. Thanks to some mousetropic calculations, he determined that there are many different dimensions in time and space, where anything could be possible.

The professor's work inspired me to write this science fiction adventure in which my family and in search We're a the spacemice.

I hope you enjoy this intergalactic adventure!

Geronimo Stilton

PROFESSOR
PAWS VON VOLT

THE SPACEMICE

GERONIMO STILTONIX

TRAP STILTONIX

THEA STILTONIX

GRANDFATHER WILLIAM STILTONIX

ROBOTIX

BENJAMIN STILTONIX AND BUGSY WUGSY

Geronimo Stilton

SPACEMICE

SLURP MONSTER SHOWDOWN

Scholastic Inc.

ISBN 978-1-338-08857-1

Text by Geronimo Stilton
Original title *Stiltonix contro il mostro slurp*
Cover by Flavio Ferron
Illustrations by Giuseppe Facciotto (design) and Daniele Verzini (color)
Graphics by Francesca Sirianni

Special thanks to Tracey West
Translated by Julia Heim
Interior design by Kevin Callahan/BNGO Books

10 9 8 7 6 5 4 3 2 1   17 18 19 20 21

Printed in the U.S.A.   40

First printing 2017

In the darkness of the farthest galaxy in time and space is a spaceship inhabited exclusively by mice.

This fabumouse vessel is called the **MouseStar 1**, and I am its captain!

I am Geronimo Stiltonix, a somewhat accident-prone mouse who (to tell you the truth) would rather be writing novels than steering a spaceship.

But for now, my adventurous family and I are busy traveling around the universe on exciting intergalactic missions.

THIS IS THE LATEST ADVENTURE OF THE SPACEMICE!

AN UNEXPLORED PLANET!

Everything was cosmically CALM when I woke up on my spaceship that morning. I left my cabin, whistling as I headed to the control room. I couldn't wait to **sink** into my captain's chair and munch on some GORGONZOLA GRANOLA, but when I got there . . .

Oh, excuse me—I haven't introduced myself. My name is Stiltonix, **Geronimo Stiltonix**, and I am captain of the *MouseStar 1*, the most mouserific spaceship in the universe!

As I was saying, as soon as I entered the control room, a THUNDEROUS voice hit my ears.

"Look lively, you **limp lunar cheese sticks**!" yelled my grandfather William Stiltonix. He was sitting in my chair, SHOUTING orders at the whole crew.

"Grandfather, how nice to SEE you," I said. "What brings you to the control room?"

Look lively!

"My feet, Grandson—and they're a lot **FASTER** than yours!" he snapped. "You're **Late** for work!"

I stammered. "B-b-but we didn't have any **missions** planned today!"

"What a lazybones!" Grandfather said. "If it were up to you, this spaceship would stay in **orbit** forever."

Before I could defend myself, **Robotix**, the ship's robot, floated over to Grandfather.

"Admiral Stiltonix, we're ready!" he said. "We have locked in the **coordinates** for our launch into hyperspace."

Launch into hyperspace? **HOLEY CRATERS!**

Hearing those words made my whiskers tremble in fright.

Entering hyperspace meant *accelerating* faster than the speed of light—which really does a number on my stomach!

"Er, Grandfather, why exactly do we need to **LAUNCH** into hyperspace?" I asked.

"Because we're **explorers**, Grandson!" he replied. "I recently identified a planet all the way at the end of the universe. It's named **Mozzarellon**, and no spacemouse has ever set paw on it. We will be the first to explore it!"

I gulped. "The end of the universe?" That sounded awfully **far away**.

But Grandfather had his mind made up. "*Full speed ahead!*" he commanded.

The ship lurched forward, and the

acceleration was so strong that I flew backward! I BUMPED my head on the floor, fainted, and began having the most **wonderful** dream . . .

In my dream, I was on the beaches of the planet **Tropicalix**. Walking next to me

was **Sally de Wrench**, the talented technician of the *MouseStar 1*—and also the most FASCINATING rodent in the galaxy . . .

A pull on my whiskers JOLTED me awake. I opened my eyes and gasped. I wasn't

Full speed ahead!

Heeeelp!

Ha, ha, ha!

looking at the kind face of Sally de Wrench—I was looking at the **goofy** face of my cousin Trap!

"Wake up, Geronimo!" he said, **shaking me** forcefully. "We've arrived at the planet Mozzarellon. It's a **mousetastic** place! We've got to get out there and explore! Come with me right now!"

A mousetastic place?
Go with him?
But why?

THE EXPLORATION MISSION

I was still **fuzzy** from bumping my head. I couldn't remember what had just happened, and I didn't **understand** what Trap was talking about. But I knew one thing for sure: I didn't want to do it!

Trap grabbed me by the **paws** and got me back on my feet.

"Cousin, what is this all about?" I snapped.

"I'll **SHOW** you," he replied.

He led me to the

Come on, Geronimo!

large monitor and showed me a planet as white as *milk*, surrounded by a cosmic cloud.

"It's the planet Mozzarellon!" he told me. "While you fainted, we launched into hyperspace and entered the planet's ORBIT!"

Then Trap typed into a keyboard and an encyclopedia entry popped up. "Look!

From the Encyclopedia Galactica
MOZZARELLON

This planet is known for its milky-white color. It has never been explored by spacemice, but visual data confirm that the surface is covered in wild mozzarella shrubs. Space probes have shown that the surface is soft and gummy. The planet's inhabitants, the cheesix, appear to resemble balls of mozzarella cheese.

There's WILD MOZZARELLA growing on the planet. We have to go check it out!"

Suddenly, I remembered Grandfather William's plans to **explore** the planet. I was trying to gather my thoughts when Trap interrupted me.

"Come on, Ger!" he urged, pushing me into the teleportation room. "The **Teletransportix** is ready to teleport us to the planet's surface! By lunchtime we'll be **ENJOYING** the first wild mozzarella in space!"

"Wait just one minute," I protested. "No mouse has ever set paw on Mozzarellon before.

We need to do some **TESTS** before we go down there. There could be GALACTIC GERMS, or **cosmic bacteria**, or space microbes . . ."

My voice trailed off when the doors of the room opened up, and in stepped **Sally de Wrench**!

Glittering galaxies, she was even more fascinating in person! I didn't want her to see how NERVOUS I was, so I turned to Trap and spoke in my most captain-like voice.

"Cousin, I would be happy

to accompany you on your exploration mission, but as **captain** of this spaceship I must stay here and do some important captain business!"

"But every **exploration mission** needs two rodents," Trap said. "How will I do it alone?"

Then something happened that I did not **EXPECT** at all.

Sally stepped forward. "Trap, I will go with you," she said.

Cheesy comets!

Was the rodent of my dreams about to go

Come on, Cousin!

I'm sorry, but I have to work!

on an exploration mission with my cousin, without me? **Was this a bad joke? A nightmare? A horror film?**

"Please, **wait** until we can do some tests," I said, but Trap and Sally ignored me. The two 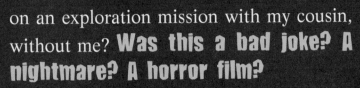 rodents were

so eager to explore Mozzarellon! They stepped into the Teletransportix and entered the planet's coordinates. Then they DEMATERIALIZED right before my eyes!

I **stared** at the empty Teletransportix for a few minutes, blinking. Then I headed back to the control room.

So far, my morning was **stinking** worse than rotten cheese!

CODE YELLOW!

I *slumped* back to the control room, disappointed in myself. I was worried that I had looked like a scaredy-rat in front of Sally!

To make matters worse, Grandfather William started yelling at me.

"What are you doing here, Grandson?" he asked. "You should be on Mozzarellon!"

I sighed. "I just think we should test for SPACE BACTERIA, and . . ."

"Tests take too much time!" said my sister, Thea. "I can't wait to get down there!"

"Really?" I asked.

Thea nodded. "I want to ride my SPACE MOTORCYCLE on the surface!"

"Did you hear that, you cheese loaf?"

Grandpa asked. "Thea has the spirit of a *true captain*!"

RED with embarrassment, I walked over to my nephew Benjamin.

He was watching Trap and Sally's mission on one of the **SCREENS** in the control room.

Benjamin SMILED at me. "Uncle, don't be worried about exploring Mozzarellon. Bugsy and I will go with you when you're done testing for space bacteria."

GALACTIC GOUDA, he is such a sweet little nephew!

I watched the screen with him. Trap and Sally were walking inside a shallow CRATER.

"Look! They found the WILD MOZZARELLA shrubs!" Benjamin cried.

The crew gathered around us, curious. Starry space dust, it was true! Growing inside the crater were strange space plants that had plump balls of mozzarella growing on their branches!

Professor Greenfur, the ship's scientist, nodded his head. "Now

this is a truly mousetastic discovery!" he remarked.

Then we heard a **Y E L L** from Hologramix, the ship's computer.

"Unidentified aliens are approaching the exploration team!

Code yellow!
Code yellow!
Code yellow!"

Thea turned on her wrist phone. "Trap, can you hear me? You need to be careful. Someone is coming toward you. It could be dangerous!"

But it was already too late. On the screen we could see Trap and Sally's terrified faces. Then Trap began to stammer.

"H-HEY, WHAT DO YOU WANT FROM US? WE'RE NOT DOING ANYTHING WRONG! HELP!"

Then the screen went blank. Total **silence** fell over the control room.

"Something tells me that those aliens weren't **friendly**," Professor Greenfur said.

My fear had frozen me like Plutonian ice. Thea shook me.

Aaaaah! *Help!*

"We've got to get down there! **There's not a moment to lose!**" she cried.

Oh, for all the shooting stars—my sister was right!

I sprang into **action** and started to quickly organize a **rescue mission**. Robotix, Thea, and I would go to the planet. Grandfather William and Professor Greenfur would coordinate the operations from **Mousestar** 1.

I stepped onto the **Teletransportix** platform with my team when Benjamin and his friend Bugsy ran up to me.

"We're coming, too!" he announced. "We've already made a **map** of this planet, so we'll be useful."

I shook my head. "No way! This could be a very **DANGEROUS** mission," I said.

But the two little spacemice **climbed** onto the platform just as Professor Greenfur activated it!

My head began to **spin** as the machine started to break apart our **molecules** into tiny pieces. Cosmic cheese chunks, what a terrible feeling!

I don't like the Teletransportix, but I had to help Trap and Sally.

I was ready for anything!

CRUSTY, RUSTY BOLTS!

We landed inside the same crater that Trap and Sally had been exploring. But *where* were they? And **WHO**—or WHAT—had scared them?

The wild mozzarella!

We began to examine the crater for clues.

Thea studied a wild mozzarella shrub. "**Amazing!** Imagine that—mozzarella growing from a bush!"

Benjamin started to **BOUNCE** up and down. "The planet's surface is soft and kind of **gummy**," he remarked.

"It's like walking on a big mattress!" Bugsy said happily.

I didn't like the bouncy surface. It was starting to make me feel **seasick**! I took a few steps and lost my balance, landing whisker-first on the ground.

Luckily, it was so **soft** that I wasn't hurt—and from down there I could see TRACKS along the bottom of the crater.

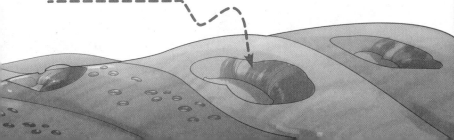

"Those are **Trap's and Sally's** pawprints!" I exclaimed.

"Good job, Ger!" Thea praised me.

We saw **smaller** tracks next to the pawprints.

"Those must be **alien** tracks!" Thea guessed.

We followed them. After a while, Trap and Sally's tracks DISAPPEARED. And the alien's footprints looked **DEEPER**.

"Hmm. What happened here?" Thea wondered. Then we heard voices.

I **JUMPED** at the noise. "That sounds like Trap and Sally!"

Thea raised a finger to her lips. "SHHH! We don't want the aliens to see us!"

We hid behind the edge of the crater and peeked out. **Shooting stars!** Trap and Sally were tied up on a pole!

The aliens who had captured them were small, round, and **chubby**. They all wore milky-white clothing. They each had two cheerful **EYES** on top of tall stalks.

"These must be the CHEESY aliens," Thea whispered. "Let's approach them carefully."

So Thea, Benjamin, Bugsy, Robotix, and I **quietly** stepped out of our hiding place and began to follow them from a safe distance.

A VERY CHEESY PLANET!

After a really LONG walk, the aliens arrived in what looked to be their capital city. We walked past houses that looked like GiaNT soft, round mozzarella balls painted in light colors.

Mousey meteorites, this was turning out to be one cheesy planet!

The cheesix led Trap and Sally into a large square, where their king was seated on a throne that almost looked like a washing machine. I could tell he was a king because he wore a CROWN on his head.

The king also wore a fancy turquoise outfit, complete with a long cloak. On either

side of his throne were large Pℓaↄↄ↑eℝS of mozzarella.

The aliens carried Sally and Trap to the foot of the throne. Then the aliens watched with **fearful** looks on their faces, waiting to hear what the king would say.

"Untie the foreigners and bring them closer!" he commanded. "I want them to bow down to **Spherus the Third**, the leader of Mozzarellon and king of the cheesix people . . . me!"

The aliens quickly untied Sally and Trap. My cousin **blurted out**, "Your Majesty, I am very hungry!"

The king frowned. He did not look pleased with Trap's **bad manners**.

"Trap, not now!" Sally hissed.

But Trap continued. "I have wanted to taste your **WiLD MOZZaRELLa** ever since I landed on this planet. **May I?**"

Without waiting for an answer, my cousin reached his paw toward one of the king's platters and grabbed a mozzarella ball! He bit into it.

"Tasty!" he exclaimed, with his mouth full. "Do you know what goes great with mozzarella balls? A touch of tomato sauce from the planet Vega. Put them together and you get a whisker-licking-good snack!"

He took a bottle of the tomato sauce from his pocket. As quick as a comet he poured some onto a mozzarella ball—and accidentally squirted some onto the king's clothes!

"Aaaaah!" shrieked the king. "How dare you dirty me with your messy sauce, stranger?!"

The king waved his scepter. "Guards, *grab him*! Take him to the Hypnotizer!"

Benjamin and Bugsy looked up at me, worried.

"Uncle, what's a hypnotizer?" Benjamin asked.

Holey craters, I had no idea! But it didn't sound good at all!

THE FOOL'S DANCE

Before we could react, **King Spherus** hopped off his throne and the aliens brought Trap over to it. The throne definitely looked like a strange **washing machine**. Apparently, it was the Hypnotizer! The aliens slipped a cap on Trap's head and connected it to the machine with a tube. Then the machine started to shoot out tiny little **BUBBLES**.

"What are they doing?" asked Benjamin, **alarmed**.

"I have discovered information about the Hypnotizer in my **Data Banks**," Robotix reported.

"What do they say?" I asked.

"The Hypnotizer is a mostly **harmless**

machine," Robotix replied.

I looked at Trap, who was SMILING. He seemed to be okay.

Thea was suspicious. "*Mostly* harmless?"

Before Robotix could answer, the machine stopped bubbling. The aliens took the strange cap off Trap's head. He blinked.

"Hey, guys, I suddenly have a strong

From the Encyclopedia Galactica
THE HYPNOTIZER

Description: Alien technology used by the cheesix of planet Mozzarellon. It causes a temporary change in personality, and the effects can wear off in as quickly as a few hours or as long as a week.
Effects: Whoever is connected to the Hypnotizer will be overcome by a strong desire to wash and iron things. It is a useful device for those who are lazy and hate to do their chores.

urge to do some housework," he said. "Do you have any spacesuits that need **washing** or **IRONING**?"

Two aliens brought Trap a big tub of **dirty** laundry. We all looked at Robotix.

"As you see, the Hypnotizer makes you want to **clean** things," Robotix said.

"These cheesix really seem to like things clean," Thea remarked.

"It's true," Benjamin said. "I don't see a **speck** of dirt on any of them."

I love to iron!

Trap was already **BUSY** at work, ironing spacesuits. We couldn't help **LAUGHING**. Normally, Trap hated doing chores!

Then King Spherus spoke up. "Since the stranger has responded so well to the Hypnotizer, let's proceed with his friend as well! **Four paws** doing the wash are better than two!"

Now, it was one thing to see Trap under the Hypnotizer's spell. But I couldn't bear to see Sally turn into a clothes-washing zombie! I ran out of my hiding place.

"Hold it right there! We are the spacemice, and we come in peace!" I yelled. "We're here to learn about your planet, not clean it!"

"What are you doing?" Thea asked.

But Sally was all I could think about.

I **RAN** toward the center of the square, yelling,

"Saaallyyy, don't be afraaaid! I'll saaave yoooou!"

I was halfway there when I **TRIPPED** on

a bump in the planet's surface! I didn't want to fall and look like a **fool** in front of Sally. Trying to keep my balance, I struck a series of **ridiculous** poses and finally landed in front of the king's throne.

What a **galactically terrible** entrance!

A Strange Resemblance

I closed my eyes, waiting for King Spherus to **yell** at me. Instead, I heard the aliens all talking at once.

"**Incredible!**" one yelled.

"**AMAZING!**" shouted another.

"**IT'S REALLY hiM!**" King Spherus exclaimed.

Then the aliens broke into **thunderous** applause, and they all bowed to me—even the king!

I was cosmically confused!

Why were they so excited?

King Spherus exclaimed, "Bring me the **Big Book of Space Legends!**"

Two aliens ran up with the book. The king took it from them.

"An ANCIENT legend says that one day a hero will arrive on our planet," he explained. "This hero will be known as the CHEESEMASTER!"

"That's a nice story," I said. "But what does this Cheesemaster guy have to do with me?"

King Spherus opened the book and showed me a picture. "The legend says that

Look here!

What do I have to do with it?

the Cheesemaster will RISK his life to save his companions. Then he will make himself known by doing a dance."

I looked at the picture in the book. JUMPING JUPITER, I really did have a strange resemblance to the Cheesemaster! And his *dance moves* in the picture looked just like the silly moves I had made when I tripped!

"SORRY, but that wasn't actually a

dance," I tried to explain, but King Spherus wasn't listening.

"We must c̶e̶l̶e̶b̶r̶a̶t̶e̶ our hero from the skies!" he announced, and the aliens all cheered.

Then the cheesix raced around, organizing a great C E L E B R A T I O N. They invited all of my friends as *honored* guests—even Trap and Sally.

Trap, surprisingly, turned down the

Hooray for the Cheesemaster!

Hooray!

invitation. "No, thank you," he said, his eyes weirdly BLANK. "I have way too much **laundry** to do." Then the aliens escorted him to an enormouse Laundromat, where he got busy washing more alien spacesuits. *Poor Trap!*

The effects of the Hypnotizer still hadn't **worn off**!

I'd rather do laundry!

A Party . . . with a Surprise!

The party was **very embarrassing** for me. The cheesix put a mozzarella necklace around my neck and began to carry me around like a **HERO**.

"Look, this is a **mistake**," I said. "I am not the Cheesemaster! I'm not a hero!"

But nobody listened to me.

As night fell, **music** began to play, and everyone

Hooray!

Um . . .

Hooray!

Hooray!

began to **dance**.
Benjamin and Bugsy had a
lot of fun, especially when
Robotix tried to teach the aliens
his favorite dance, the ROBOT
SHUFFLE.

The cheesix were CONFUSED at first, but
they picked it up quickly.

As it turns out, the cheesix were very **good dancers**, and they could dance all night without stopping. And **guess who** they wanted to dance with? Me!

I danced and danced until my fur was **FRAZZLED** and my whiskers were **DROOPING**. The cheesix didn't understand how **tired** I was.

Party on!

Dance with me!

Umm . . .

Me too!

No, me first!

"Cheesemaster, don't you like the music?" one asked me. "We can put on **Taylor Swiss**! Or do you like space rap? How about some Chee-Z?"

I COULDN'T TAKE IT ANYMORE!

I marched up to King Spherus on my tired paws.

"Your Majesty, when does the dancing end?" I asked. "My muscles are as wobbly as string cheese!"

"You can go to sleep now, Cheesemaster," the king replied. "Tomorrow you have a busy day!"

"Busy?" I asked, suspicious.

"Tomorrow you will complete the **second part** of the prophecy," King Spherus answered, smiling. "That's when the Cheesemaster challenges the Slurp Monster to a duel and frees our people!"

DUEL? SLURP MONSTER?!

I broke out into a cold sweat. My whiskers began to **TREMBLE** in fright.

"Slurp Monster?" I asked.

"The Slurp Monster lives on the other side of our planet," the king explained. "He

Ooh, the horror!

is a **horrible**, **GIANT**, furry monster!"

"M-m-monster?" I stammered.

King Spherus nodded. "The monster spends most of his time **sleeping**. But when he wakes up, he comes out of his cave and stomps on our MOZZARELLA bushes — then slurps up way more mozzarella than he needs! He STOMPS and *slurps* until he's exhausted, and then he goes back to sleep."

"And how exactly do you expect my brother to DUEL this monster?" Thea asked.

"He's the HERO — he should know," the king replied. "And when he wins, he can tell the monster not to bother us anymore."

Great galaxies, what a NiGhTMaRE!

I didn't want to **fight** a monster. I wasn't the Cheesemaster — but none of the aliens believed me. There was only one thing I could do: rUN!

I didn't get very far before the king's **guards** surrounded me.

"Take him to the **luxury** space cell!" King Spherus commanded. "We must treat the Cheesemaster well, but we must also make sure he doesn't rúñ off. We've waited two hundred years for him to arrive!"

Umm . . .

You're not going anywhere!

I'm Not a Warrior! I'm Not!

That's how I ended up in a luxury space apartment—one with B A R S on the door and windows!

I huddled on my bed, SHAKING like a spacequake.

"Oh, for a million moons! How am I supposed to duel a giant monster? I'm not a WARRIOR. I'm a space captain who would rather be a full-time writer!" I wailed.

All I could think about was the horrible Slurp Monster, who would surely reduce me to space dust in an astrosecond!

Suddenly, I heard a voice from the window.

What will I do?

"Geronimo! We're here!"

I turned and **saw** Thea with Benjamin, Bugsy, Sally, and Robotix!

I **jumped** up. "How great to see you!" I exclaimed, relief washing over me. "How did you **find** me?"

"It was easy," Thea replied. "After all that dancing, the cheesix fell into a **deep sleep**."

"The whole city is *snoring*, including the king!" Sally continued. "So it was simple to follow the guards without being noticed."

"And we found a way to **help** you, Uncle," Benjamin added.

I brightened up. "Really? You can get me out?"

"Well, not exactly . . . " Thea replied, her voice trailing off.

Sally nodded. "Actually, Captain, we don't have the technology to deactivate the LASER bars in your cell."

"So then how are you going to help me?" I asked in a tiny voice.

Benjamin pulled a small **gadget** from his pocket. It looked like a piece of cheese. He passed it to me through the bars.

"We can help you **DEFEAT** the monster," he said.

I turned as **PALE** as mozzarella.

"We contacted the *MouseStar 1*,"

What is it?

It's a flash drive!

Benjamin went on. "Hologramix gathered all known data on the **SLURP MONSTER** and put it on this flash drive for you. If you connect it to your wrist computer, you can see all the information."

Bugsy nodded. "We discovered that the monster has a few weaknesses," she said. "You can STUDY them as you prepare for the duel."

I couldn't believe it. "But I'm not a warrior! What good will it do me to know my monster's weaknesses if I faint as soon as I see him?"

"You have no choice, Ger," Thea said.

I sighed. "All right. I promise I will do my best."

I needed to get to work. I didn't have much time to learn all the secrets of the **SLURP MONSTER**!

THE POWER OF TICKLING!

Thea and the others left, and I **inserted** the flash drive into my wrist computer. **Rays of light** shot from the watch and quickly began to take shape. Blinking, I watched as two rodents whom I knew **very well** appeared before me.

"Professor Greenfur? Grandfather? What are you doing here?" I asked.

"I knew you would fall for it like

a **cheesehead**, Grandson!" Grandfather William replied in a booming voice. "We're not real! What you are seeing is a **three-dimensional** image of us, PROJECTED from your wrist computer!"

I reached out to touch them, but my paw passed right *through* them as though they were cosmic clouds. They were **holograms**, just like Hologramix back on the ship!

"I'm CONFUSED," I said. "I thought the

Grandfather? Professor?

You cheesehead!

flash drive contained data about the Slurp Monster, not you!"

"WE'VE got the data for you," Grandfather replied. "Thea tells me that you're afraid to duel this monster. Is that right?"

"Well, basically . . ." I began.

"You're as soft as cream cheese!" Grandfather barked. "You need to buck up and act like hard cheese, like a sharp cheddar!"

"So you want me to act like cheese?" I asked, confused.

At that point, an image of the Slurp Monster *projected* from my wrist. Professor Greenfur began to speak.

"As you can see, the Slurp Monster has six arms and one big eye," he began.

I gulped. "And one enormouse mouth!"

"They are very **RARE** creatures," Professor Greenfur continued. "In fact, only one or two can be found in each galaxy. Despite their terrible appearance, they are not as **TOUGH** as they look. They have a major **weak spot**."

Now I was curious. "What's their weak spot?"

"They are extremely **ticklish**!" the professor replied.

Cosmic cheddar, those beasts were ticklish? I couldn't believe it.

"There is one way to **defeat** this monster," Professor Greenfur went on. "Allow the creature to grab you. Just before you are swallowed up, tickle it with a **feather**."

"Did you say I should let it **GRAB ME**?" I asked nervously, but the professor ignored me.

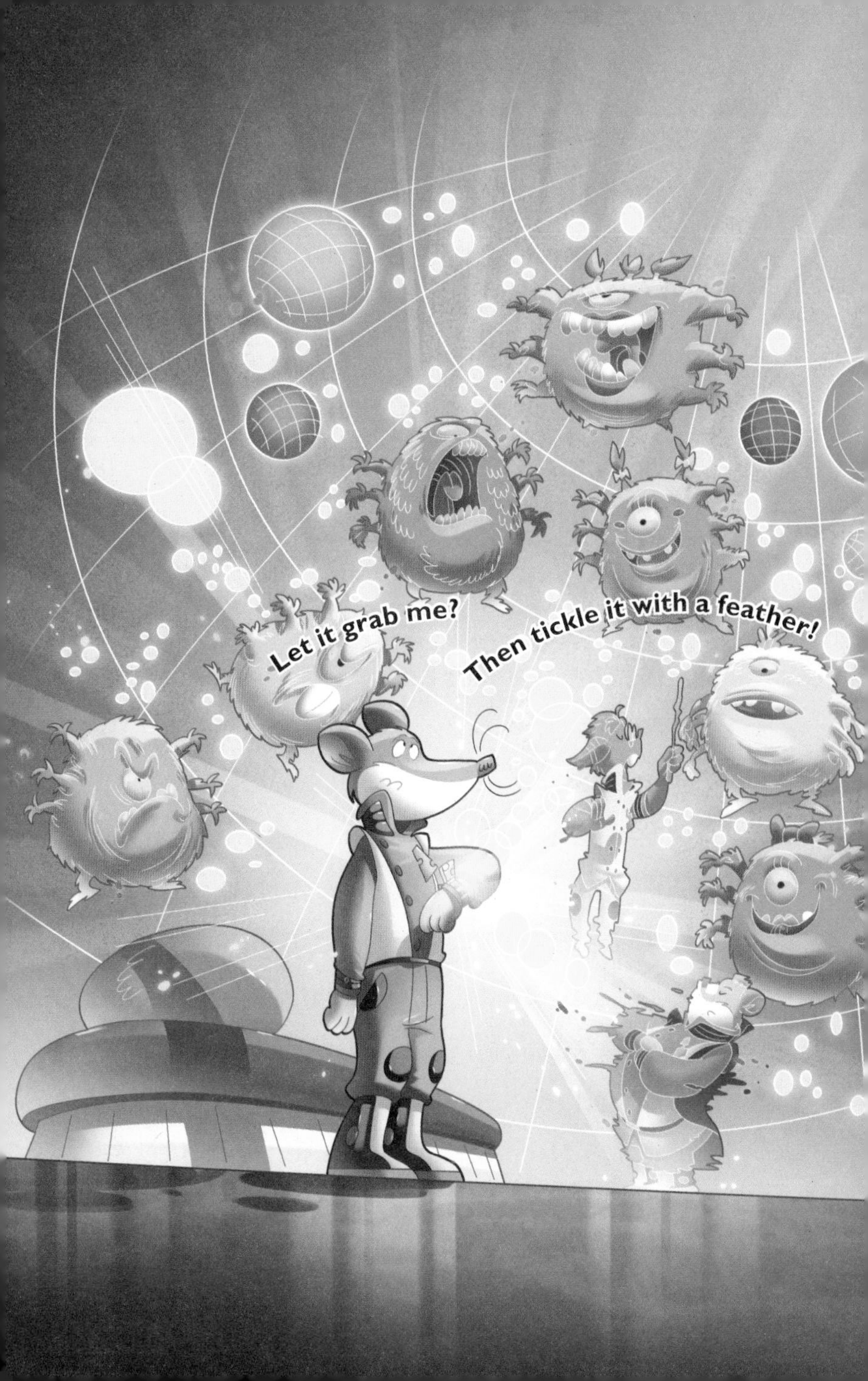
Let it grab me?
Then tickle it with a feather!

"If this maneuver is carried out correctly, the monster will start LAUGHING and give up the duel," Professor Greenfur explained.

"So **listen up**, Grandson!" Grandfather barked. "Tomorrow, when the duel begins, Thea will toss you a feather. The rest should be as **easy** as taking cheese nuggets from a baby rodent."

I frowned. Tickling a GIANT space monster didn't sound easy to me!

"Our time is up," Grandfather said. "Hologram projection will drain the battery life of your wrist computer pretty quickly. Behave like a **true captain** tomorrow, you hear?!"

The images faded, and I was alone in my cell. I tried to sleep, but images of the Slurp Monster *danced* in my worried mind . . .

When I did fall asleep, I had terrible

nightmares that the Slurp Monster grabbed me and **gobbled** me down in one bite!

Galactic Gorgonzola, how scary!

SNORE . . . RUMBLE!

The next morning, **KING SPHERUS** and a group of guards came to get me.

"Cheesemaster, did you sleep well?" the king asked. "Are you ready for the **big duel** with the Slurp Monster?"

"Actually, I TOSSED and **turned** all night," I replied. "I was too **afraid** to sleep!"

The king burst out laughing. "Ha! That's a good one,

Yawn . . .

Hey there!

Cheesemaster. I like a hero with a **sense of humor**."

I knew there was nothing I could say to convince him that I was not a HERO, so I didn't say anything. The guards led me out of my cell and brought me to a small space shuttle. We departed for the other side of the planet, where the monster lived.

During the trip I looked out the window and saw that a space shuttle from the *MouseStar 1* was following us. I kept my snout shut, because I knew that my **friends** were behind me! That gave me a bit (but just a bit) of courage.

When we landed, the ground began to shake . . .

"Just what we need—a SPACEQUAKE!" I yelled.

"That's not a spacequake, Cheesemaster,"

King Spherus said, amused. "It's just the Slurp Monster, **SNORING**! His snores are so strong they make the ground **RUMBLE**."

Shooting stars! The Slurp Monster was **bigger** than I'd realized!

I thought maybe I could use the situation

to my ADVANTAGE. "If the monster is snoring so hard, maybe this isn't the best time to wake him," I suggested. "We might just make him **angry**."

"The Slurp Monster is always angry," King Spherus replied. "Anyway, I know

Snore . . . Rumble

Spacequake!

a trick that can help you **defeat** the monster."

"**A trick?**" I asked hopefully. "Well, that changes everything. What is it?"

King Spherus frowned. "You're pretty **impatient** for a hero, Cheesemaster. I'll tell you when the time is ready."

I sighed. The king just didn't get it. I wasn't impatient . . .

I was frightened out of my fur!

A Rude Awakening

We stepped out of the shuttle in front of a large cave.

"That is where the Slurp Monster **sleeps**," King Spherus explained.

My whiskers were **trembling** with fright as we stepped inside the dark cave. There, snoring away, was the giant SLURP MONSTER! He was even more **terrifying** in person.

The guards approached him and began to shake him to wake him up. But the monster kept snoring.

"Use a long stick to pry open his eye!" the king ordered.

The guards prodded the monster's EYE, but he just started snoring LOUDER than before.

"Maybe we should just leave," I suggested.

The king ignored me. "Use the **space resonator**!" he commanded.

The cheesix put a machine that looked like an *enormouse trumpet* up to the monster's ear. Then . . .

Ooooooeeeeee!
Ooooooooeeeeee!

The resonator let out a sound like a siren. The monster opened his eye and let out a terrible R⊘AR!

"Galactic Gorgonzola, I told you he would get **ANGRY**!" I squeaked, running out of the cave.

The others followed me, and the **monster** stomped out behind us. He looked like he was in a **terrible mood**.

The king and his guards FLED, leaving me

by myself. As I saw the king run away, I
remembered something.

"Your Majesty, WAIT! You didn't tell
me the trick to defeating the monster!" I
yelled after him.

The king stopped. "Oh right, I forgot.
Legend says that the monster will only be

defeated when the hero yells, 'Give up, you one-eyed fur ball!' Now excuse me, Cheesemaster, but I must be Running off!"

I couldn't believe my ears. That was the trick? Yelling an INSULT? That didn't sound like such a GOOD idea to me.

The king and his guards boarded the space shuttle and flew away.

Stinky space cheese, they had left me all alone!

I tried to remember what Professor Greenfur had told me. And the king's trick. But my mind was as BLANK as a slice of provolone.

I was so SCARED I couldn't think straight!

I was done for . . .
        finished . . . hopeless!

I was frozen with fear. The Slurp Monster grabbed me with one hand and lifted me into the air. The words the king had said popped into my brain.

"Give up, you one-eyed fur ball!"

But the words only made the monster **ANGRIER**! He growled and started to **SQUISH** me like a mozzarella ball!

I needed another plan if I wanted to **KEEP MY FUR**!

Grrr! Grrr!

SHAKEN LIKE A SWISS CHEESE SMOOTHIE!

"Hang tight, Geronimo, we're here!"

HOPE returned as I heard Thea's voice. She, Benjamin, Bugsy, Sally, and Robotix came *RUNNING* toward me.

The Slurp Monster reached for them with his other five hands. They all **dodged** him. Thea jumped between two 𝔣𝔲𝔯𝔯𝔶 hands and yelled, "Geronimo, this is for you! You can do it!"

Then she threw me a colorful feather.

I hesitated. The king's trick hadn't worked. What if tickling made the monster even **anGRieR**?

I closed my eyes, imagining the monster gobbling me down like a jalapeño popper. When I opened them, I saw that the monster had grabbed everybody!

"Help us, Uncle Geronimo!" Benjamin pleaded.

Seeing that the rodents (and robot) I cared about most were in danger gave me COURAGE. I grabbed the feather and yelled, "Let go of my friends or you'll have to deal with me!"

Then I began to brush the feather against the monster's head. He stopped growling. His massive belly started to shake, and he closed his mouth to keep himself from laughing. His one giant eye started to tear up.

"Keep doing it, Geronimo. It's working!" Thea urged me.

"Yeah, he's in trouble now!" Bugsy cheered.

I waved the feather even **FASTER** and the monster started to **swell up** as he tried hard to hold back his laughter.

Holey craters, it looked like he was about to **BURST**!

I thought I had **WON**, but I was wrong . . .

Mmmmmmfff!

Tickle, tickle, tickle . . .

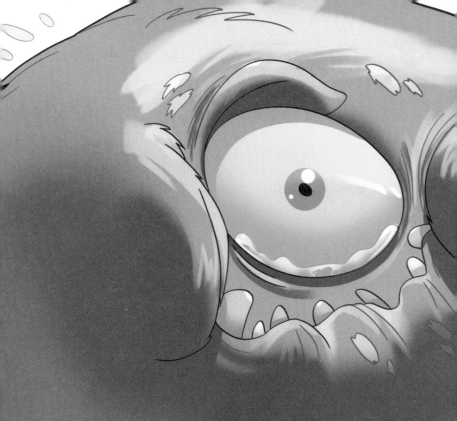

Unfortunately, he managed to hold back his laughter. He **shook me** like a Swiss cheese smoothie! My insides were starting to feel **scrambled**!

All that shaking **knocked** the feather out of my paw. I watched it FLOAT slowly to the ground.

Nooooooooooo!

Then the monster lifted me above his **ENORMOUSE** mouth and opened it wide. Believe me, friends, I have never been so AFRAID in all my life . . .

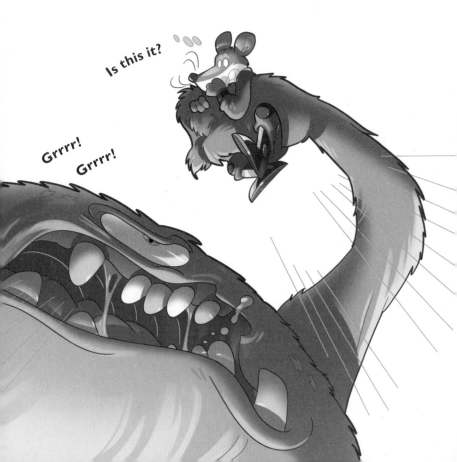

Is this it?

Grrrr!

Grrrr!

MONSTROUS
EMOTIONS

Stinky space cheese, I had to try something!

I grabbed the monster's finger and started shaking my paw at him. "Let me go, you big mound of fur!" I yelled.

The SHAKING activated my wrist computer. It began to project the 3-D images of the Slurp Monsters that Professor Greenfur had sent me.

The monster's eye grew WIDE when he saw the other monsters. Then he let out a big sigh and let go of me and the others! We fell to the ground. Thump!

Luckily, the surface of the planet

Mozzarellon is soft and B°UNCY, so we didn't get hurt. We looked at one another, **stunned**. We couldn't believe we were free!

"For all the short circuits, why did the monster give up so suddenly?" ROBOTiX asked.

"I have no idea!" I responded.

But Benjamin and Bugsy were both *smiling*—they had figured it out.

"It's obvious, Uncle G!" Benjamin said. "Look at his face. That **giant furball** is emotional!"

Emotional? Is that possible?

When I looked at the monster, I knew Benjamin and Bugsy were right.

The monster's **angry** expression had completely changed. His face was SWEET and **sad**.

"Of course!" Sally exclaimed. "The Slurp Monster is all alone on this planet. Seeing the images of the other monsters is making him feel Sad. That's why he let us go!"

"I don't think he's actually evil at all. I just think he's **lonely**," Bugsy said.

I understood what they meant. **Underneath that mountain of muscles, the monster had a heart!**

Galactic Gouda, who would have guessed?

I could have **ESCAPED** then with my friends and never looked back. But the monster was so sad. And the cheesix would still have a monster **PROBLEM**. I couldn't just leave, could I?

Then an iDEa hit me.

"What if we help this monster find his friends?" I suggested. "If he were happier, he might stop TERRORIZING the cheesix by stomping and slurping their mozzarella bushes."

Benjamin and Bugsy looked at each other.

"We have an idea," Benjamin said. "Follow us!"

And so we all boarded the space shuttle and quickly returned to the *MouseStar 1*.

ULTRAGIGATONIC POWER!

When we reached the *MouseStar 1*, Benjamin and Bugsy **ran** to look for Professor Greenfur. The rest of us followed them to the professor's lab.

"Welcome back! What can I do for you?" he greeted us.

Bugsy had to catch her **breath** before she could talk. "We need to know if you can modify the Teletransportix to transport something that is VERY LARGE!" she blurted out.

"And very FAR AWAY!" Benjamin added.

Professor Greenfur frowned. "It depends on what you have in mind," he said.

"We think the *Slurp Monster* stomps and slurps the mozzarella bushes because he's ANGRY that he's all alone, and he's bored," Benjamin explained. "So, if we could transport other Slurp Monsters to Mozzarellon, he might be **happier** and stop destroying the mozzarella."

"That's a great idea, Benjamin!" I said.

But Professor Greenfur was still frowning.

"This can't be done easily," Professor

What do you have in mind?

We have an idea!

Greenfur explained. "To **dematerialize** all the molecules of a Slurp Monster, you would need ultragigatonic power. Our Teletransportix only has **regular** gigatonic power."

The room went silent as we looked at one another, DISAPPOINTED. Benjamin and Bugsy's plan was great — but how could we make it happen?

"Wait, I have an idea!" Sally exclaimed suddenly. "The SOLUTION might be right under our snouts. The *MouseStar 1* engine has ULTRAGIGATONIC POWER! Working together, Professor Greenfur and I could temporarily transfer all of the POWER of the spaceship to the Teletransportix."

Bugsy grinned. "Then it would have enough energy to transport a Slurp Monster!"

Didn't I tell you that Sally was brilliant?

"Excellent thinking, Sally!" Professor Greenfur cried. "There is no time to lose. **Let's get to work!**"

Sally and Professor Greenfur quickly began to do calculations.

"We need to get to the control room," Thea said. "We've got to locate other Slurp Monsters in the universe!"

So Thea, Benjamin, Bugsy, Robotix, and I *HURRIED* to the control room, **excited** about the new plan.

HARDER, GERONIMO!

I **BURST** into the control room first.

"Hologramix, locate all monsters similar to the **slurp monster** that are present in the universe!" I called out. "Get me their coordinates as quickly as possible so we can teleport them. We are on an **URGENT** mission to . . ."

That's when I noticed that the control room was **D A R K**. None of the machines were humming. Then a **flashlight beam** appeared out of the darkness. It was my grandfather!

"What are you **blabbering** on about, Grandson?" Grandfather asked. "I don't know what **MESS** you made in the laboratory, but we've lost all

ELECTRICITY! Nothing works!"

"Of course!" Thea cried. "Professor Greenfur and Sally have transferred all the **energy** from the *MouseStar 1* to the Teletransportix. But we should have asked them to wait. We need **power** so we can locate the **MONSTERS**!"

What have you done?

Grandfather shook his head. "It's the *same old story*. Once again, it's up to me to get you all out of trouble! Luckily, when they built the *MouseStar 1*, I made them put in an old energy generator that will always work in an emergency."

"What kind of generator?" I asked.

Grandfather pulled a lever on a control panel, and a TRAPDOOR on the floor opened up. Holey craters, I had no idea that hiding place existed!

Then he pulled out a STRANGE contraption. It looked like a bicycle, with pedals and two **wheels**, linked by cables to a battery. He set it up in front of me.

"Here you go, Geronimo!" he said. "Start pedaling!"

It looked like it would take a lot of pedaling to generate enough energy to get the control room operating.

"Maybe we should talk to Professor Greenfur," I suggested. "There must be some **other way** to—"

"There you go, Grandson, acting like soft cheese again," he scolded me. "You said so yourself: All the ship's energy is needed to power the Teletransportix. What, are you **afraid** of a little hard work? A little SWEAT?"

"N-no, Grandfather," I stammered.

Thea stepped up. "I'll do the pedaling," she offered.

"No!" Grandfather barked. "**This is a job for the ship's captain!**"

"Maybe we could **take turns**?" I suggested, but Grandfather wasn't hearing it.

"Hop on that machine **right now**, Geronimo!" he yelled.

I tried one more plea. "But, Grandfather, **I haven't trained, I'm not ready, and I'm not good at it!**"

But Grandfather just **GLARED** at me, and I climbed on the generator with a sigh. Then I began to pedal.

"FASTER, YOU MOLDY MANCHEGO!" Grandfather yelled. "We need more energy!"

Faster, you moldy Manchego!

Oof!

His **booming** voice spurred me on, and I pedaled faster. In a few minutes, the **LIGHTS** in the control room came on. The machines began to hum.

"HOORAY!" everyone cheered.

But I wasn't cheering. I still had to pedal faster . . . and faster . . . and faster . . . and I couldn't stop until we located the monsters!

MONSTER MOLECULES APPROACHING!

Now that Hologramix had power, it began searching for Slurp Monsters. After a few **astroseconds**, it made an announcement.

"All the similar **Slurp Monsters** of the universe have been identified!"

"Good work! Show us images on the screen," Grandfather said.

HOLOGRAMIX obeyed. We saw that every Slurp Monster was alike. No matter what planet they were on, each monster was angrily **stomping** around, destroying stuff, and **slurping** it up.

"There's no time to lose," Thea said. "We

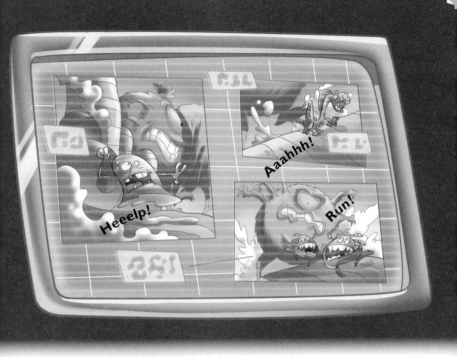

need to **transport** all of them!"

But I was starting to think the plan was a bad idea. "What if they all behave like this on Mozzarellon? We'll be causing even more **TROUBLE** for the cheesix!"

"Uncle, trust me," Benjamin whispered. "I looked the Slurp Monster in the eye and understood that he wasn't bad, just very *lonely*. I am sure that is the same for the others."

I looked into my nephew's kind *eyes* and knew I had to trust him.

"**Prepare the Teletransportix!**" I shouted, still pedaling furiously. "We will relocate each of the monsters to Mozzarellon. Hologramix, send the **coordinates** to Professor Greenfur!"

Sally turned on the Teletransportix, and immediately, beams of GOLDEN LIGHT shot out in all directions. We watched the **screen** to see what would happen.

One by one, the monsters **disappeared** as their molecules dematerialized. The aliens on the planets all CHEERED to see the monsters go.

"I think you made the right decision, Ger," Thea said.

"I hope so," I replied, and then Robotix said exactly what I was thinking.

"We cannot celebrate just yet," he said. "Right now, millions of MONSTER MOLECULES are approaching Mozzarellon. We still do not know what will happen when the monsters arrive."

I was almost AFRAID to find out. What if we were wrong? MOZZARELLON MIGHT BE DESTROYED!

A Friend Is a Treasure

We hopped back into the space shuttle and headed to Mozzarellon. We wanted to be there when the MONSTERS arrived.

When we landed, we saw a group of the Slurp Monsters gathered near the city of the cheesix. They all looked SURPRISED at first. But when they saw each other, they smiled and started hugging one another!

"See? They look HAPPY," Benjamin remarked.

King Spherus marched toward us. "Cheesemaster, what is going on? You were supposed to defeat the Slurp Monster, not bring us more!"

"But look," Thea said. "They're not stomping or slurping anymore. They're just **HUGGING**."

"The Slurp Monster was just *LONELY*," Benjamin piped up. "Now that he has **friends**, he won't bother you anymore."

The Slurp Monsters all **NODDED** to show they agreed.

"No more stomping and slurping?" King Spherus asked. "Why, that's *wonderful*! I knew you could do it, Cheesemaster! Thank you!"

"You're welcome," I said. "And now, we really should be GOING . . . "

"NONSENSE!" the king cried. "The cheesix will honor our **HEROES** with three days of dancing and celebration!"

DANCING? CELEBRATION?

THREE DAYS?! AGAIN?!

HEEEEEEELP!

I tried to protest, but it was too late. The party had already started!

And that's how, once again, I was forced to **DANCE** for three straight days! The monsters joined the celebration as well, and quickly became **friends** with the cheesix. It felt great to see that our plan had worked out so well!

I was **exhausted** when the party finally ended, and I was glad that

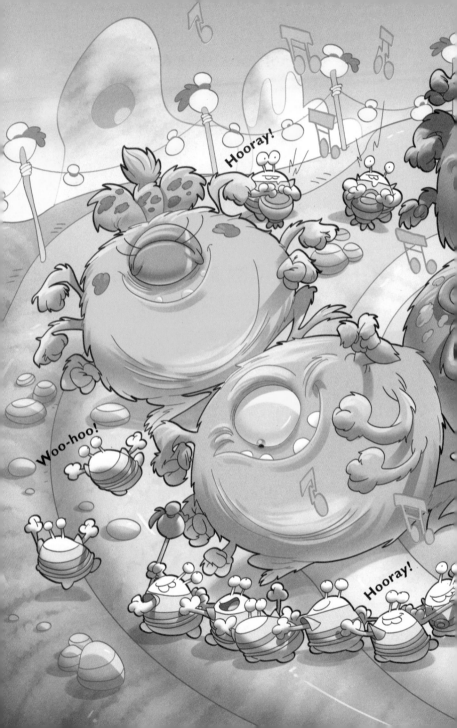

it was time to **depart**. A happy crowd accompanied us to the shuttle that would return us to the *MouseStar 1*.

As we climbed on board, we heard a cry.

"Hey, don't leave *without me!*"

It was my cousin **Trap**. Holey craters, we had almost **forgotten** about him!

The effects of the **Hypnotizer** had finally worn off, and Trap had returned to **normal**. He climbed on board the shuttle, scratching his head.

Don't forget me!

"I really don't remember how I ended up in that enormouse **Laundromat** doing all that cleaning," he said. "Tell me, did I miss anything **important**?"

We all laughed, and Benjamin and Bugsy filled

him in on what had happened.

Then the shuttle docked with the ship, and we headed to the control room, where Grandfather William was waiting for us.

"It's about time, you CHUNKS OF COSMIC CHEDDAR!" he said. "We still have so many corners of the universe to explore! And you, Grandson, tell me: Did you LEARN anything from this adventure?"

I thought for a moment. "Yes," I replied. "I learned that friendship is the best tool in the cosmos for solving conflicts."

"Well done, Grandson!" Grandfather said, patting me on the back. "You actually did a pretty GOOD JOB with this mission. You are not a total cheesebrain!"

The words filled me with joy. Grandfather almost never complimented me!

But his good mood didn't last long.

"We've **WASTED** enough time!" he boomed. "Let's get navigating. **Full speed ahead!**"

The MouseStar 1 zipped away from Mozzarellon, heading toward a new **astral** adventure. But that's a story for another day. See you next time!

Don't miss any adventures of the Spacemice!

#1 Alien Escape

#2 You're Mine, Captain!

#3 Ice Planet Adventure

#4 The Galactic Goal

#5 Rescue Rebellion

#6 The Underwater Planet

#7 Beware! Space Junk!

#8 Away in a Star Sled

#9 Slurp Monster Showdown

Up Next!

#10 Pirate Spacecat Attack

Be sure to read all my fabumouse adventures!

#1 Lost Treasure of the Emerald Eye

#2 The Curse of the Cheese Pyramid

#3 Cat and Mouse in a Haunted House

#4 I'm Too Fond of My Fur!

#5 Four Mice Deep in the Jungle

#6 Paws Off, Cheddarface!

#7 Red Pizzas for a Blue Count

#8 Attack of the Bandit Cats

#9 A Fabumouse Vacation for Geronimo

#10 All Because of a Cup of Coffee

#11 It's Halloween, You 'Fraidy Mouse!

#12 Merry Christmas, Geronimo!

#13 The Phantom of the Subway

#14 The Temple of the Ruby of Fire

#15 The Mona Mousa Code

#16 A Cheese-Colored Camper

#17 Watch Your Whiskers, Stilton!

#18 Shipwreck on the Pirate Islands

#19 My Name Is Stilton, Geronimo Stilton

#20 Surf's Up, Geronimo!

#21 The Wild, Wild West

#22 The Secret of Cacklefur Castle

A Christmas Tale

 **#23 Valentine's Day Disaster**

 **#24 Field Trip to Niagara Falls**

 **#25 The Search for Sunken Treasure**

 **#26 The Mummy with No Name**

 **#27 The Christmas Toy Factory**

 **#28 Wedding Crasher**

 **#29 Down and Out Down Under**

 **#30 The Mouse Island Marathon**

 **#31 The Mysterious Cheese Thief**

 **Christmas Catastrophe**

 **#32 Valley of the Giant Skeletons**

 **#33 Geronimo and the Gold Medal Mystery**

 **#34 Geronimo Stilton, Secret Agent**

 **#35 A Very Merry Christmas**

 **#36 Geronimo's Valentine**

 **#37 The Race Across America**

 **#38 A Fabumouse School Adventure**

 **#39 Singing Sensation**

 **#40 The Karate Mouse**

 **#41 Mighty Mount Kilimanjaro**

 **#42 The Peculiar Pumpkin Thief**

 **#43 I'm Not a Supermouse!**

 **#44 The Giant Diamond Robbery**

 **#45 Save the White Whale!**

 **#46 The Haunted Castle**

#47 Run for the Hills, Geronimo!

#48 The Mystery in Venice

#49 The Way of the Samurai

#50 This Hotel Is Haunted!

#51 The Enormouse Pearl Heist

#52 Mouse in Space!

#53 Rumble in the Jungle

#54 Get into Gear, Stilton!

#55 The Golden Statue Plot

#56 Flight of the Red Bandit

The Hunt for the Golden Book

#57 The Stinky Cheese Vacation

#58 The Super Chef Contest

#59 Welcome to Moldy Manor

The Hunt for the Curious Cheese

#60 The Treasure of Easter Island

#61 Mouse House Hunter

#62 Mouse Overboard!

The Hunt for the Secret Papyrus

#63 The Cheese Experiment

#64 Magical Mission

#65 Bollywood Burglary

The Hunt for the Hundredth Key

#66 Operation: Secret Recipe

MEET
Geronimo Stiltonord

He is a mouseking — the Geronimo Stilton of the ancient far north! He lives with his brawny and brave clan in the village of Mouseborg. From sailing frozen waters to facing fiery dragons, every day is an adventure for the micekings!

#1 Attack of the Dragons

#2 The Famouse Fjord Race

#3 Pull the Dragon's Tooth!

Don't miss any of these exciting Thea Sisters adventures!

Thea Stilton and the Dragon's Code

Thea Stilton and the Mountain of Fire

Thea Stilton and the Ghost of the Shipwreck

Thea Stilton and the Secret City

Thea Stilton and the Mystery in Paris

Thea Stilton and the Cherry Blossom Adventure

Thea Stilton and the Star Castaways

Thea Stilton: Big Trouble in the Big Apple

Thea Stilton and the Ice Treasure

Thea Stilton and the Secret of the Old Castle

Thea Stilton and the Blue Scarab Hunt

Thea Stilton and the Prince's Emerald

Thea Stilton and the Mystery on the Orient Express

Thea Stilton and the Dancing Shadows

Thea Stilton and the Legend of the Fire Flowers

Thea Stilton and the Spanish Dance Mission

Thea Stilton and the Journey to the Lion's Den

Thea Stilton and the Great Tulip Heist

Thea Stilton and the Chocolate Sabotage

Thea Stilton and the Missing Myth

Thea Stilton and the Lost Letters

Thea Stilton and the Tropical Treasure

Thea Stilton and the Hollywood Hoax

Thea Stilton and the Madagascar Madness

Meet
GERONIMO STILTONOOT

He is a cavemouse — Geronimo Stilton's ancient ancestor! He runs the stone newspaper in the prehistoric village of Old Mouse City. From dealing with dinosaurs to dodging meteorites, his life in the Stone Age is full of adventure!

#1 The Stone of Fire

#2 Watch Your Tail!

#3 Help, I'm in Hot Lava!

#4 The Fast and the Frozen

#5 The Great Mouse Race

#6 Don't Wake the Dinosaur!

#7 I'm a Scaredy-Mouse!

#8 Surfing for Secrets

#9 Get the Scoop, Geronimo!

#10 My Autosaurus Will Win!

#11 Sea Monster Surprise

#12 Paws Off the Pearl!

#13 The Smelly Search

#14 Shoo, Caveflies!

Don't miss any of my adventures in the Kingdom of Fantasy!

THE KINGDOM OF FANTASY

THE QUEST FOR PARADISE:
THE RETURN TO THE KINGDOM OF FANTASY

THE AMAZING VOYAGE:
THE THIRD ADVENTURE IN THE KINGDOM OF FANTASY

THE DRAGON PROPHECY:
THE FOURTH ADVENTURE IN THE KINGDOM OF FANTASY

THE VOLCANO OF FIRE:
THE FIFTH ADVENTURE IN THE KINGDOM OF FANTASY

THE SEARCH FOR TREASURE:
THE SIXTH ADVENTURE IN THE KINGDOM OF FANTASY

THE ENCHANTED CHARMS:
THE SEVENTH ADVENTURE IN THE KINGDOM OF FANTASY

THE PHOENIX OF DESTINY:
AN EPIC KINGDOM OF FANTASY ADVENTURE

THE HOUR OF MAGIC:
THE EIGHTH ADVENTURE IN THE KINGDOM OF FANTASY

THE WIZARD'S WAND:
THE NINTH ADVENTURE IN THE KINGDOM OF FANTASY

THE SHIP OF SECRETS:
THE TENTH ADVENTURE IN THE KINGDOM OF FANTASY

MouseStar 1

The spaceship, home, and refuge of the spacemice!

MouseStar 1
(exterior view)

1. Control room
2. Gigantic telescope
3. Greenhouse to grow plants and flowers
4. Library and reading room
5. Astral Park, an amousement park
6. Space Yum Café
7. Kitchen
8. Liftrix, the special elevator that moves between all floors of the spaceship
9. Computer room
10. Crew cabins
11. Theater for space shows
12. Warp-speed engines
13. Tennis court and swimming pool
14. Multipurpose technogym
15. Space pods for exploration
16. Cargo hold for food supply
17. Natural biosphere

Dear mouse friends,
thanks for reading,
and good-bye until the next book.
See you in outer space!